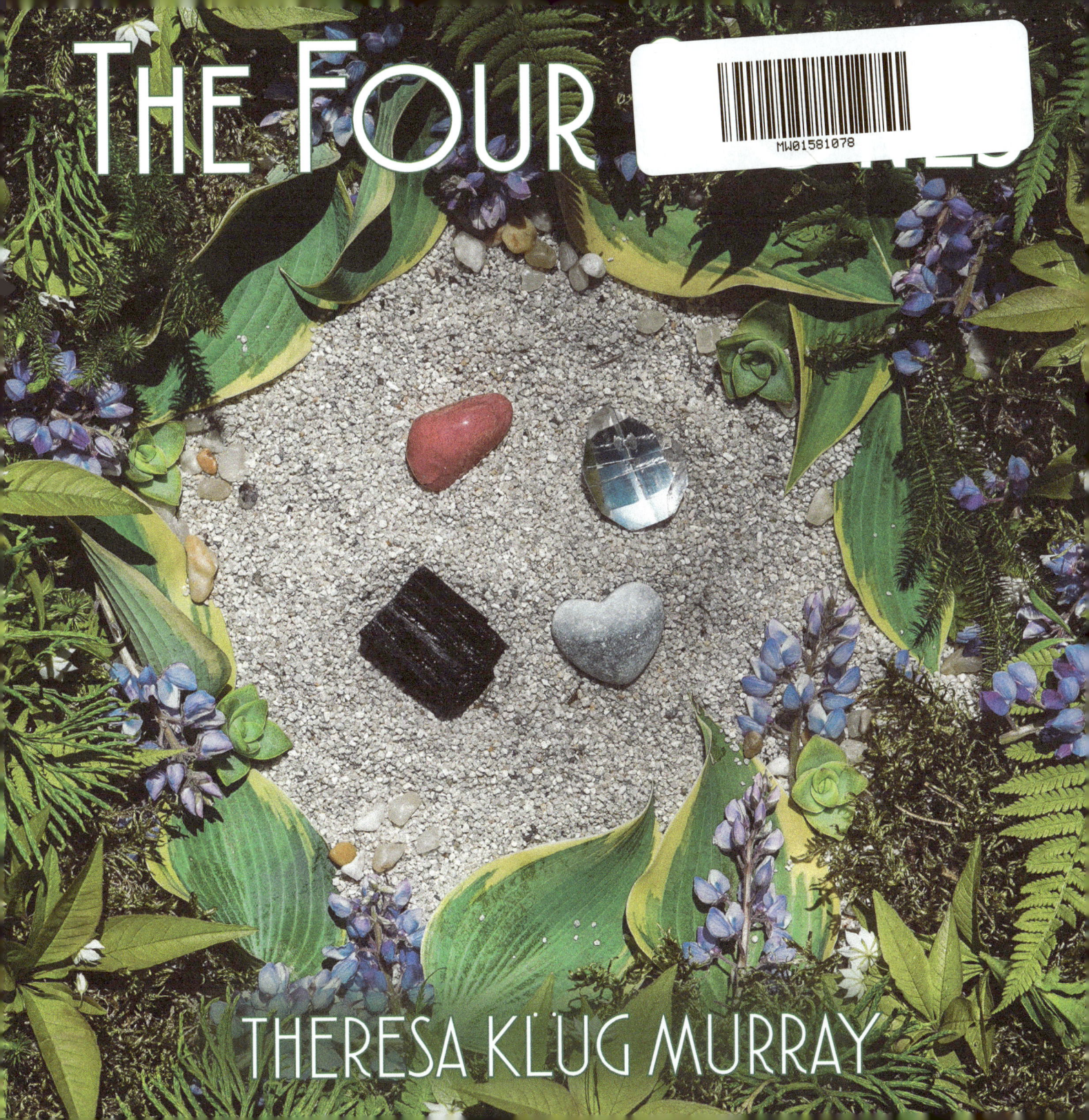

The Four Stones copyright 2021 by Theresa Klüg Murray
All rights reserved. This book or any portion thereof
may not be reproduced or used in any manner whatsoever
without the express written permission of the publisher
except for the use of brief quotations in a book review.

First printing: July 2021
ISBN: 978-1-952976-22-3
Library of Congress Number: 2021913730
Printed in the United States of America
Published by Kirk House Publishers

Illustrated by: Theresa Klüg Murray and Patty Klüg Miller
Photographed by: Irvin Segura

Kirk House Publishers
1250 E 115th Street
Burnsville, MN 55337
612-781-2815

This book is dedicated to you, the reader.
May you be reminded often of the Great Creator's eternal love for you.
May you feel The Creator in the Wind, the Woods, the Weeds and in one another.

In memory of Ed and John.

Early one spring, Peep and Chip poked their little-bird heads from their little-bird eggs to sing to the morning sun. They were greeted by the Great Creator, who placed around their necks four small stones.

The first stone was called Joy and sparkled brightly in the sun's rays. This stone was gifted with Imagination, Light, and Wonder and tied firmly in place by a thin wool thread.

The second stone, called Hope, was smooth and colorful. The Creator gifted it with Imagination and Dreams.

The third stone, Will, contained the gifts of Strength, Determination, and Courage.
It was dark like the night
and shone like glass.

Now, the fourth stone was different from the others. It was not bright, colorful, or shiny, yet it was far more precious than the other three. This stone was called Love.

The Creator tenderly tied a Love stone around each of their necks by a thin golden thread. "This stone," he explained, "contains my deep love for you and all of creation. It never fades nor gives up. It binds us all together
and lasts forever."

Many happy days went by that summer for Peep and Chip. They soared happily on warm breezes and played among the forest with their friends Squirrel, Rabbit, Fox, and Owl.

One morning, as the days grew short and the leaves began to dress in their best colors, Peep and Chip flew high into the clouds. Suddenly, a fierce wind whipped wildly at the little birds. Chip's stones tangled together, breaking the string that held the Joy stone, and whisked it far away.

Surprised, Chip noticed that without the stone, his wings became weak and heavy because Laughter, Light, and Wonder no longer lifted him high. Still, they journeyed on.

Peep led Chip to a calm forest where they could flutter from tree to tree. Before long, a sharp branch caught the stone called Hope from around Chip's neck. It tugged mightily at the string until it snapped, leaving him unable to see. Without Imagination and Dreams, Chip lost his way and tumbled to the ground. Still, they journeyed on.

Peep and Chip rested peacefully on a winding path near a quiet river. Wanting to share her Joy and Hope with Chip, Peep whistled songs and told stories to remind him of their forest adventures while the sun set low in the sky.

In the early morning light, while Peep was fast asleep, Chip stretched his wings and hopped along the winding path until he wandered into a thicket of thistles.

The tiny thorns snagged, scratched, and shredded the thread belonging to the Will stone until, at last, it broke free and slipped deep into the thorny weeds.

The last of Chip's Strength, Courage, and Determination slipped away. Now only his Love stone remained. Chip rested quietly. Knowing he was safe in the Creator's everlasting love, he breathed deeply for the very last time.

And then, his Spirit journeyed on.

Chip found himself nestled safely in the Creator's palm. Glancing down, he saw that his three lost stones were securely fastened around his neck along with his Love stone. He was once again filled with Joy, Hope, and Will. Chip wondered how they had gotten there.

Smiling kindly, the Creator explained, "Little friend, I was with you in the wind and among the branches and even in the thorns. I have given you new stones. These stones will last forever."

Whistling sweetly, Chip flapped his wings
and flitted through the fresh air.
He dove and circled until he
was dizzy. Resting again in the Creator's hand,
he sighed, "Peep will be sad and lonely when
I am not there with
her to play in the forest."

Tenderly, the Creator replied,
"I will send your forest
friends to help her along the way.
I will always be with her too.
Remember, my Love is deep. It never
fades nor gives up. It binds us together forever."

Smiling up at the Creator, Chip nodded
his head, flapped his wings, and sang his song.
And so, they journeyed on.

The sounds of chattering friends surrounded Peep in the rays of the morning sun.

The Creator had gifted Squirrel with a Servant's Heart, and so he brought Peep seeds and berries to give her strength.

The Creator had gifted rabbit with long Compassionate ears for listening, and so Peep shared her feelings until she felt light again.

Next, the fox wrapped his long, soft tail around Peep. Comfort was the gift given to him by the Creator. Peep felt the hug of its gentle warmth.

At last, Owl, who was full of wisdom, stretched her wings wide and raised her head knowingly. "My brave little friend," she said, "someday we will see Chip again. If we share the Creator's love, we are never really separated from him."

Looking around, Peep understood what the Creator had said that early spring morning, long ago. His love binds us all together. It never fades nor gives up, and it lasts forever. Hope quietly found its way into Peep's heart.

And so, connected by the Great Creator's love, they all journeyed on.

Guided questions for discussion

The Creator gives Peep and Chip Joy, Hope, and Will.

How would you describe those gifts?

- What brought joy to your loved one?

- What dreams and hopes did your loved one have?

- When did your loved one show strength, determination, and courage?

- Can you think of other "stones" that your loved one had?

How does the Creator describe the Love stone?

- Imagine your loved one with you right now. Describe your love to him or her.

- How do you think your loved one would describe his or her love for you?

The birds spent their summer making memories with their forest friends.

- What are your favorite memories of your loved one?
- What can you do today to keep those memories alive?

In losing his Joy, Hope, and Will, Chip also lost his Strength and Health. What kinds of difficult experiences were part of your loved one's journey?

- How did your loved one respond to those experiences?
- How did it affect other people in his or her life?
- Describe how it affected you.

Peep tried to help Chip regain his hope and joy by sharing memories.

- Make a list of people who surrounded your loved one and describe ways in which they helped.
- What did you notice about how he or she responded?

It is important to talk about your loved one's passing, even when it hurts. Take some time now to share your feelings from when you learned that he or she had journeyed on.

- Draw a picture or write down some of the emotions you felt on that day.

Reread the pages in which Chip journeys to be with the Creator and talk about what jumps out at you.

- What examples of the Creator's love do you notice in this story?
- In what ways do you think the Creator helped your loved one?
- What beliefs does your family have about the afterlife?
- Do you believe your loved one has been restored? If so, what might that look like?

In the final pages of the story, we notice that Peep's friends offer their gifts to her.

- Who do you know that has similar gifts to Squirrel, Rabbit, Fox, and Owl in your life?
- How have those gifts helped you?
- What gifts has the Creator given you? Who needs the Creator's love the most right now and how can you share God's love with them?

Throughout this story, we notice that Peep, Chip, the forest friends, and the Creator have been on this journey together, connected by the Creator's great love.

- Describe what you imagine heaven will be like when your journey leads you there.
- If you could pick one adventure to have with your loved one when you meet again, what would it be?
- What are some things you can do right now to feel connected to your loved one until you meet again?
- If you are ready, take some time to talk to God, the Creator, about your hopes and dreams and your sadness, and ask Him to be a part of your journey.

God's promises through His word: 1 John 4:16

                                 Matthew 10:29-31

                                 1 Corinthians 13:7, 8 and 13

                                 2 Corinthians 4:16-17

                                 Lamentations 3:22-23

About the Author

Theresa Klüg Murray grew up in a large, close knit family that is rich in love for God, each other and nature. Working as a nurse in the school setting for 25 years, she has witnessed many young students experience the death of loved ones. Recent personal experiences of death by suicide and death associated with addiction have called her to write her first children's book.

The Four Stones is a story designed to illustrate death in a way that is easy for children to understand. It includes guided questions to generate conversations with their families and caregivers as they navigate the emotional journey through grief.

Theresa has felt the Spirit of God partnering with her throughout the writing of this book. Finding her inspiration in nature she co-created the illustrations with her talented sister and son-in-law. It is her desire to point readers to the limitless love of God so that they may find hope and healing within its pages.

Theresa and her husband, Bryan, live in Prescott, Wisconsin. They currently love watching their two married children become parents and pursue their dreams. Between their faith, the great outdoors and grandchildren, their cups are overflowing.

Lightning Source UK Ltd.
Milton Keynes UK
UKHW051130300821
389697UK00005B/27

9 781952 976223